This edition published by Parragon Books Ltd
in November 2017 and distributed by

Parragon Inc.
440 Park Avenue South, 13th Floor
New York, NY 10016
www.parragon.com

Copyright © Parragon Books Ltd 2013–2017

Written by David Bedford
Illustrated by Brenna Vaughan and Henry St Leger
Edited by Laura Baker
Designed by Ailsa Cullen
Production by Rob Simenton

ISBN 978-1-5270-0975-2

Printed in China

I love my Mommy

PaRragon

Bath • New York • Cologne • Melbourne • Delhi
Hong Kong • Shenzhen • Singapore

One morning, Little Deer didn't want to
play around his home anymore.
"I want to see new things,"
he told his mommy.
"Then let's go exploring," said Mommy Deer,
"and see what new things we can find."

"This way!" said Little Deer excitedly,
and he hurried ahead, while Mommy followed
behind, watching over him.

Little Deer **hopped** along the grass by the hanging willow tree. Then he slowly crossed the wobbly stones, watching the stream as it trickled gently beside him.

"Don't get your feet wet," warned Mommy.

"I won't!" said Little Deer, as he

wiggled
and
wobbled.

Little Deer counted red and orange butterflies, then squeezed through thick, tangly bushes.

"Don't get stuck," warned Mommy.

"I won't!" called Little Deer, as he skipped out the other side.

"Hurry up, Mommy!" he called. "There's so much more to see."

"Look!" said Little Deer.
"A hill that goes up to the clouds!"
"Is it too high?" said his mommy.

"It's not too high for me,"

said Little Deer, panting as he climbed step by step all the way to the top.

"I can see **forever!**"
cried Little Deer, standing tall
on his tiptoes.

His mommy stood close beside
him, but Little Deer was
beginning to wobble again,

and suddenly . . .

"Wheeee!"

cried Little Deer as he
skidded and slid, landing
with a swoosh in a pile of
fallen leaves.

"Are you okay, Little Deer?"
asked his mommy.

"Yes!" giggled Little Deer. "I am!"

Little Deer sat in the meadow with his mommy, watching the bees buzzing in the warm sun.

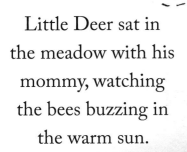

Suddenly, Little Deer sat up. "Mommy?" he said. "Which way is home?" He looked all around him.

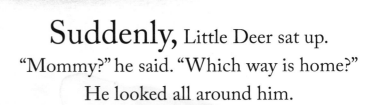

"I'm lost!"

Mommy Deer nuzzled Little Deer's nose. "We'll soon find our way back," she said soothingly. "We just have to remember how we got here."

Little Deer thought and thought. At last, he began to remember . . .

"We came over the hill!"
cried Little Deer, and he
scampered back to the hill that
went up to the clouds.

Mommy Deer helped him climb
quickly to the top, where . . .

"Yippee!"

cried Little Deer. "I can see the way from here!"

Little Deer and his mommy skidded down the other side of the hill to find what came next.

"We squeezed through the tangly bushes!" Little Deer told his mommy, and he scurried back through the hole he'd made, with his little tail wagging. Mommy Deer gave him a helping nudge.

"Which way now?" said Little Deer's
mommy, when they were on the other side.
Little Deer saw the red and orange butterflies, and
heard the trickling sound of a stream . . .

"The wobbly stones!" cheered
Little Deer, as he hurried across the stream.

"Don't get your feet wet, Mommy," he warned.

"I won't!" laughed Mommy Deer.
"But who's going to be
home first?"

Little Deer knew the way from here.

He ran as fast as his little legs would take him, along the grass by the willowy tree until . . .

"I'm
home
first!"

said Little Deer,
and he jumped and
jumped all around
his little yard.

Little Deer flopped down in the sunshine beside Mommy.

"I love exploring," said Little Deer happily.

"And I love
my mommy!"